This Little Tiger Book Belongs To:

_____

_____

_____

_____

LITTLE TIGER PRESS
An imprint of Magi Publications
1 The Coda Centre, 189 Munster Road
London SW6 6AW
www.littletigerpress.com

This paperback edition published 2001
First published in Great Britain 2000

Originally published in Germany 1998 by
Baumhaus Verlag, Frankfurt

Text and illustrations © 1998 Klaus Baumgart
English text © 1999 Little Tiger Press

All rights reserved • Printed in Singapore

ISBN 1 85430 683 9

3 5 7 9 10 8 6 4 2

Laura's Christmas Star

Klaus Baumgart

English text by Judy Waite

LITTLE TIGER PRESS

London

"Do you believe in magic?" asked Tommy, watching Laura pack her suitcase. They were going to Aunt Martha's for Christmas this year. Laura smiled.
It was a quiet, secret smile.
"Sometimes," she said.
"Aunt Martha says her Christmas tree looks magical," Tommy went on. "She says it's huge and sparkly and it glitters like a zillion stars. I can't *wait* to see it."

"Are you packed?" asked Mum, coming into the room. She gave them both a hug. "It's time for bed now. Otherwise you'll both be tired and grumpy on the journey to Aunt Martha's tomorrow."

Laura closed her eyes, letting pictures of a zillion glittery stars float into her thoughts.

"Is it morning yet?" asked Tommy.

Laura opened one eye.

"We've only just gone to bed," she said. "Go back to sleep."

Laura closed her eyes again and thought of huge sparkly Christmas trees and colourful crackers.

"Is it time to get up yet?" asked Tommy.

"Not nearly," said Laura. "It's still the middle of the night."

Ten minutes passed. It seemed like ten years to Tommy.

"Is it morning *now*?" asked Tommy, nudging Laura awake.

Laura opened both her eyes. She seemed to have slept a long time. "I think it must be," she said.

Laura and Tommy jumped up, pulled on their clothes,
and ran into Mum and Dad's bedroom.
"It's not time to get up," groaned Mum, waking up.
"Go back to bed!"
Laura and Tommy wandered back to their room, but they
didn't go to bed. They sat by the window, staring out at
the zillions of sparkly, glittering stars.
"Look!" cried Tommy, pointing. "That star's brighter than
the others."
Laura smiled her secret smile. The bright star was her own,
special, magic star. She had once rescued it when it had
fallen from the sky. When it was better, she had set it free.
But though it was now far away, she knew it was her friend.

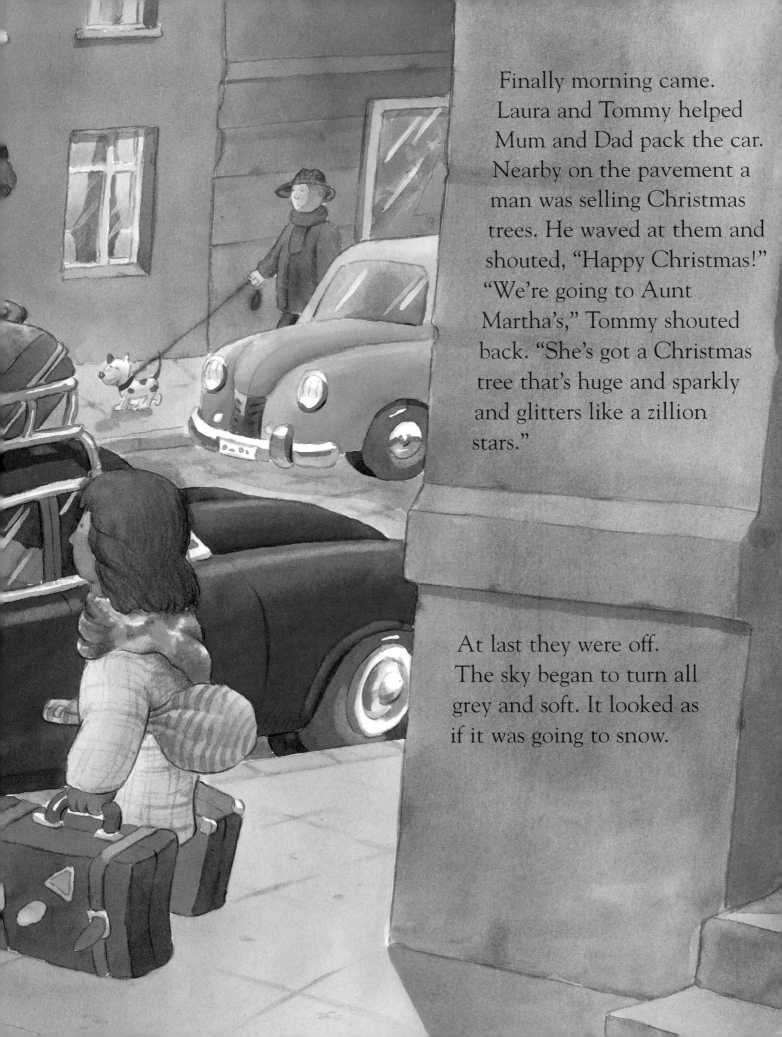

Finally morning came. Laura and Tommy helped Mum and Dad pack the car. Nearby on the pavement a man was selling Christmas trees. He waved at them and shouted, "Happy Christmas!" "We're going to Aunt Martha's," Tommy shouted back. "She's got a Christmas tree that's huge and sparkly and glitters like a zillion stars."

At last they were off. The sky began to turn all grey and soft. It looked as if it was going to snow.

As they reached the country, beautiful snowflakes began to drift down. Laura and Tommy pressed their noses against the car window and watched them cover the earth like icing on a Christmas cake.

Suddenly, the car began to rattle. It began to cough.

"It sounds like it's got a bad cold," said Laura.

"It sounds like it's broken down," said Mum.

Everyone got out, and Dad opened up the bonnet.

He pulled at some wires, but he didn't get the car started.

Everyone climbed back into the car and waited for the
repair man to arrive. It grew colder and colder,
and everyone huddled together to keep warm. Dad tried
singing Christmas songs and telling jokes, but the songs
sounded flat, and the jokes weren't funny.
"I'll tell you a story," said Laura. "It's about a magic
Christmas star that saves everybody."
But as she started, Tommy began to cry. "There's no such
thing as magic," he whispered sadly. "We'll *never*
get to Aunt Martha's now. I'll never see her huge sparkly
Christmas tree that glitters like a zillion stars."

By the time the repair man had
mended the car it was too late to go to Aunt Martha's.
Tommy tried not to cry as Dad drove back home and they
carried their suitcases into the house.

Tommy stayed sad as the daylight faded and the night crept
back into the sky.

"I wish I could do something to make Tommy happy again,"
Laura whispered. She looked out of her bedroom, and her
special star appeared. It shone down at her, as if it
understood Tommy's sadness.

The man who had been selling Christmas trees had long
since gone, but suddenly Laura noticed that he had left
behind a little tree. It lay in the snow looking ragged and
battered, and very lonely. "I'll get it for Tommy," Laura
cried. "Maybe it will cheer him up."

Laura ran outside to where the little tree
was lying. "Come indoors with me," she
said. "You look awfully lonely out here
on your own."

Laura carried the tree into the house.
"Thanks for getting it," said Tommy sadly. "It's a nice little tree, but it's not very sparkly, is it? It's not very glittery."
Laura looked at the tree. Tommy was right.
It could never be like the magical tree Aunt Martha had promised them.
Laura went upstairs to sit by her window. At least she could tell her star how helpless she felt. It always listened to her and understood. But as she looked into the night sky, she gasped with horror. Her special star had disappeared!

Now Laura was as sad as Tommy. There wasn't much
to feel happy about now she had lost a special friend.
And maybe Tommy was right. Maybe there was no
such thing as magic after all.
Suddenly, she heard Dad calling to them.
"Laura, Tommy, come here quickly!"
Puzzled, the two children trailed downstairs.
"Look!" gasped Mum, as they all stood by the living
room door.
Laura and Tommy looked. They couldn't believe what
they were seeing.
"It's *wonderful!*" cried Tommy, turning to Laura with
shining eyes. "But how could it have happened?"

Laura smiled her quiet, secret smile.
She knew, of course. "It must be magic,"
she said.

The Very Noisy Night
Diana Hendry · Jane Chapman

Fireman PiggyWiggy
Christyan and Diane Fox

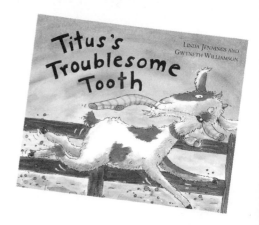

Titus's Troublesome Tooth
LINDA JENNINGS AND GWYNETH WILLIAMSON

Enter the magical world of
LITTLE TIGER PRESS

Little Bear's Grandad
Nigel Gray · Vanessa Cabban

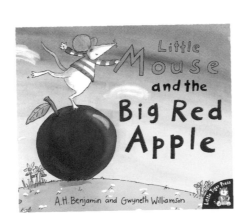

Little Mouse and the Big Red Apple
A.H. Benjamin and Gwyneth Williamson

A peekaboo riddle book
who's that scratching at my door?
Amanda Leslie

For information regarding any of the above titles or for our catalogue, please contact us: Little Tiger Press, 1 The Coda Centre, 189 Munster Road, London SW6 6AW, UK. Telephone: 020 7385 6333 Fax: 020 7385 7333 e-mail: info@littletiger.co.uk • www.littletigerpress.com